Letter from the Translators

Dear Readers,

We frequently bring our talk "The Magical Encounter Between Books and Children" to readers' communities, and wherever we are, we try to introduce children to books. When a child has found a friend in the pages of a book, that child is already on the path to academic success.

Professionally, we come from the fields of applied linguistics and education, areas in which we have published extensively and on which we have lectured in universities around the world. Personally, we are both daughters of the imagination and friends of discovery. As children's authors we have published hundreds of books, and because we are bilingual, we love to share the treasures hidden in the books of English and Spanish speaking authors, which we had an opportunity to do as consultants on the Green Light Readers/Colección Luz Verde series.

It was a pleasure to select these excellent stories with great illustrations for beginning readers and make them available in Spanish in words as engaging as those used in the originals. For the Spanish-speaking child, it will be significant to have access to authentic texts by recognized authors and illustrators in the United States. For the child learning Spanish, it is essential for the language to be not only correct but inspiring.

The early experiences between children and books are key to their future success. Opening the door of wonder, magic, fun, and knowledge through the printed word is the first step for children in loving the world that reading will bring to their lives. With bilingual books, a universal mind can be fostered at very early ages. That is the world our children will need, and we are helping them to get there.

¡Felicidades!

Alma Flor Ada & F. Isabel Campoy

Tumbleweed Stew
Sopa de matojos

Susan Stevens Crummel

Illustrated by/Ilustrado por

Janet Stevens

Translated by/Traducido por

F. Isabel Campoy y Alma Flor Ada

Green Light Readers   Colección Luz Verde

sandpiper

Houghton Mifflin Harcourt

Boston   New York

Jack Rabbit opened his eyes. He stretched and looked up at the pretty blue sky.

Juan Conejo abrió los ojos. Se estiró y miró al precioso cielo azul.

Jack's tummy growled. He thought,
The sun is up. The sky is blue!
What a great day for tumbleweed stew!
He hopped along, jumping over brush
and cactus.

A Juan le sonaron las tripas. Pensó:
El cielo azul y el sol brillante en mis ojos.
¡Qué día perfecto para una sopa de matojos!
Y se fue saltando sobre matas y cactus.

Before long, he came to a big gate. Over the gate it said TWO CIRCLE RANCH. Jack slipped under the fence and into a herd of cattle.

Al poco rato llegó al portón de una cerca. Arriba decía: RANCHO DE LOS DOS CÍRCULOS. Juan se coló bajo la cerca y se encontró en medio de una manada de vacas.

"Moo!" said Longhorn. "Move on!"
"Well, howdy," Jack said. "How do you do?
How would you like some tumbleweed stew?"

—¡Muu! —dijo Cuernoslargos—. ¡Vamos,
vete de aquí!
—¡Vaya, muy buenas! —dijo Juan—. ¿Cómo
está usted? Le gustaría un poco de sopa de
matojos?

"There's no such thing as
tumbleweed stew," said Longhorn,
munching the dry grass.

—¡No existe tal cosa! ¿Qué es eso de sopa
de matojos? —dijo Cuernoslargos mien-
tras seguía comiendo hierba seca.

Not a nice place, thought Jack. He ran down the path to the ranch house. "Anyone home?" he called. "*No!*" he heard from inside. "Go away!" "How about some lunch?" asked Jack.

No es un buen sitio éste, pensó Juan. Y corrió sendero abajo, a la casa del rancho. —¿Hay alguien aquí? —preguntó. —¡No! —oyó decir desde el interior—. ¡Lárgate!

Armadillo came out onto the porch. "This is my ranch," she said. "This is my food and you can't have any!"

Armadillo salió al portal.
—Este rancho es mío —dijo—.
¡Esta comida es mía y no vas ni a probarla!

Jack took a chance. He said,
"But I would like to cook for *you*.
Have you heard of tumbleweed stew?"
"There's no such thing as tumbleweed stew," Armadillo said.

Juan se arriesgó y dijo:
—Pero me gustaría cocinarte algo.
¿Has oído hablar de la sopa de matojos?
—¡No existe tal cosa! ¿Qué es eso de sopa de matojos? —dijo Armadillo.

Before Armadillo could blink, Jack started
a fire. He spied an old pot and filled it with
water. He set the pot of water on the fire.
After a while, he stuffed a big tumbleweed
into the pot.

Antes de que Armadillo pudiera pestañear
siquiera, Juan había encendido un fuego.
Llenó de agua una vieja cazuela. La puso al
fuego. Al cabo de un rato echó
un matojo a la cazuela.

Armadillo looked into the pot. Jack took
a taste and said,
  "It smells so good. It tastes good, too.
   But it needs more, this tumbleweed stew."
"Well," said Armadillo. "There might be some
carrots in my house."

Armadillo le echó un vistazo a la cazuela.
Juan probó el caldo y dijo:
—Huele muy bien. Y además sabe muy bien.
Pero esta sopa de matojos necesita algo más.
—Bueno —dijo Armadillo—, puede que en
mi casa haya unas zanahorias.

Soon the tumbleweed
Muy pronto los matojos

and carrots
y las zanahorias

were cooking
in the big pot.

se cocían
en la gran cazuela.

Buzzard floated down to take a look. "I can smell this food way up in the sky! It needs onions," he said. "I'll fly home and get some."

Buitre planeó bajo para echar un vistazo. —¡Se puede oler esta comida desde lo alto del cielo! Necesita cebollas—dijo—. Vuelo a casa y las traigo.

Soon the tumbleweed,
Muy pronto los matojos

carrots,
las zanahorias

and onions
y las cebollas

were cooking in the big pot.
se cocían en la gran cazuela.

Then Deer trotted over and looked into the pot. "This stew needs corn," he said. "I'll be right back."

Entonces, Venado se acercó de un salto y miró al interior de la cazuela.
—Esta sopa necesita maíz —dijo—. Ya vengo.

Soon the tumbleweed,
Muy pronto los matojos

carrots,
las zanahorias

onions,
las cebollas

and corn
y el maíz

were cooking in the big pot.
se cocían en la gran cazuela.

Skunk scampered up to the pot. "Smells good," she said. "But where are the potatoes? I'll go dig some up."

Zorrillo correteó hasta la cazuela. —Huele bien —dijo—. Pero, ¿dónde están las papas? Voy a sacar unas cuantas de la tierra.

Soon the tumbleweed,
Muy pronto los matojos

carrots,
las zanahorias

onions,
las cebollas

corn,
y el maíz

and potatoes
y las papas

were cooking in the big pot.
se cocían en la gran cazuela.

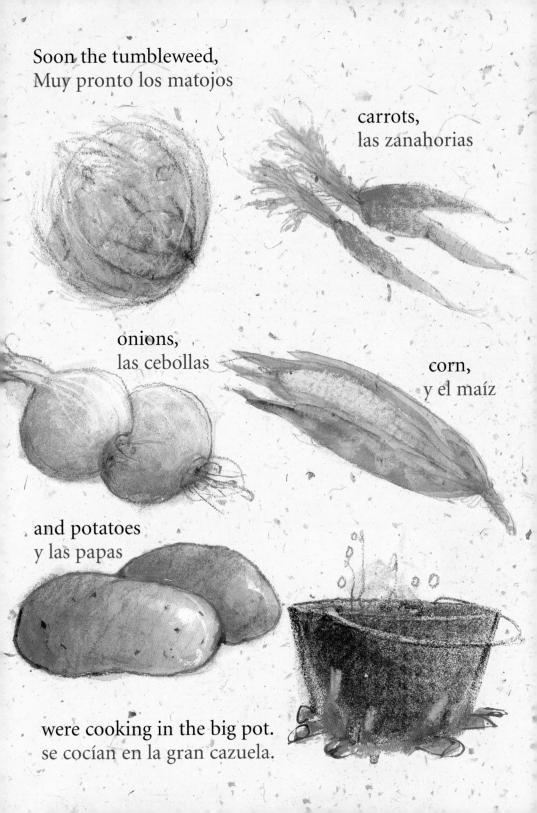

Rattlesnake slithered over with some celery. "You can't make stew without celery," he said.

Serpiente de cascabel llegó arrastrando un poco de apio. —No se puede hacer una sopa sin apio —dijo.

Soon the tumbleweed,
Muy pronto los matojos

carrots,
las zanahorias

corn,
el maíz

onions,
las cebollas

potatoes,
las papas

and celery
y el apio

were cooking in the big pot.
se cocían en la gran cazuela.

Armadillo, Buzzard, Deer, Skunk, and
Rattlesnake gathered around the pot of
stew. They watched it bubble and steam.

Armadillo, Buitre, Venado, Zorrillo y
Serpiente de cascabel se reunieron alrede-
dor de la cazuela. Miraron cómo la sopa
hacía burbujas y echaba humo.

At last Jack cried,
  "It took a while, but thanks to you,
    It's time to eat this tumbleweed stew!"
The animals ate and ate until every bite of
stew was gone.

Por fin, Juan Conejo gritó:
      —Costó un poco, pero gracias a ustedes es
hora de tomarse esta sopa de matojos.
Los animales comieron y comieron hasta que no
quedó ni una gota de sopa.

Armadillo couldn't move. Buzzard couldn't fly.
Deer couldn't trot. Skunk couldn't scamper.
Rattlesnake couldn't slither.
They put their heads down and fell asleep.
Jack slept, too, but not for long.

Armadillo no se podía mover. Buitre no podía
volar. Venado no podía trotar. Zorrillo no podía
corretear. Serpiente de cascabel no podía
deslizarse.
  Se recostaron y se durmieron.
  Juan durmió también, pero no por mucho rato.

Jack Rabbit opened his eyes. He stretched
and looked up at the pretty blue sky.
His tummy growled. He thought,
  Another day for being sly—
  What a great day for cactus pie!

Juan Conejo abrió los ojos. Se estiró y miró al
precioso cielo azul.
Le sonaron las tripas. Pensó:
Otro día para ser astuto . . .
¡Qué día perfecto para un pastel de cactus!

Think About It

1 How does Jack Rabbit get the other animals to put vegetables in the stew?

2 Would you want to have Jack Rabbit for a friend? Why or why not?

3 What did you learn about the characters from looking at the pictures? What else do the pictures tell you?

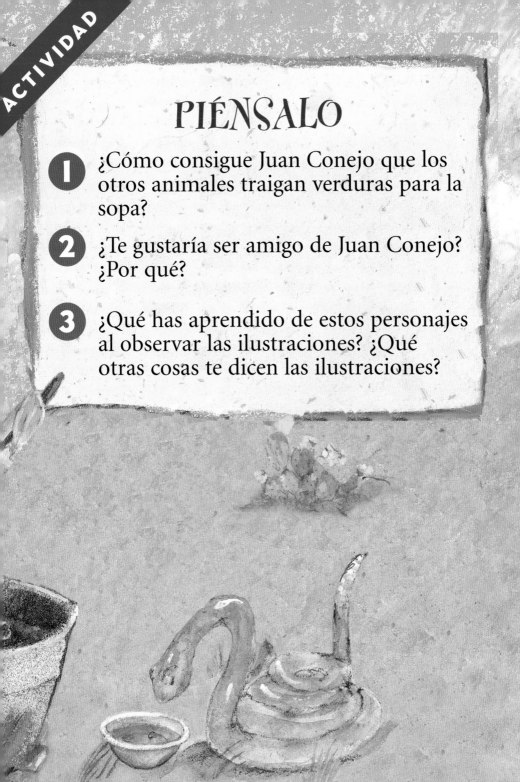

PIÉNSALO

1 ¿Cómo consigue Juan Conejo que los otros animales traigan verduras para la sopa?

2 ¿Te gustaría ser amigo de Juan Conejo? ¿Por qué?

3 ¿Qué has aprendido de estos personajes al observar las ilustraciones? ¿Qué otras cosas te dicen las ilustraciones?

Make a Tumble-Snack

WHAT YOU'LL NEED

pretzels    raisins   popcorn    nuts

small plastic
bags   measuring
cup   large self-closing
plastic bags

3 cups popcorn

1 cup nuts

2 cups pretzels

2 cups raisins

- Measure each ingredient and pour them into a large plastic bag.

- Close the bag. Shake the bag to "tumble" your snack.

- Pour or scoop out the snack into small bags.

Now eat your delicious

Tumble-Snack!

HAZ UNA MERIENDA DE MATOJOS

Lo que necesitas

pretzels

pasas

palomitas de maíz

nueces

bolsitas de plástico pequeñas

una taza para medir

bolsas grandes de plástico con cierre

3 tazas de palomitas de maíz

1 taza de nueces

2 tazas de pretzels

2 tazas de pasas

- Mide los ingredientes y échalos todos juntos en una bolsa grande de plástico.

- Cierra la bolsa. Sacude la bolsa para mezclar tu merienda.

- Echa el contenido en bolsitas pequeñas.

Ahora, ¡cómete tu deliciosa

merienda de matojos!

Meet the Author and Illustrator

Susan Stevens Crummel and her sister, Janet Stevens, grew up all over the United States, including Texas, where *Tumbleweed Stew* takes place. The sisters worked together on the story. Susan wanted the characters in the story to be animals that live in Texas. Janet kept drawing them until she liked the way they looked. "The best part of making this story was working with my sister," says Janet.

Conoce a la autora y a la ilustradora

Cuando eran niñas, Sara Stevens Crummel y su hermana Janet Stevens vivieron por muchos lugares de los Estados Unidos incluyendo Texas, donde ocurre *Sopa de matojos*. Las dos hermanas trabajaron juntas para crear este cuento. Susan quería que los personajes fueran animales de los que viven en Texas. Janet los fue dibujando hasta que te gustaron. "Lo mejor de crear este cuento fue trabajar con mi hermana", dice Janet.

About the translators

F. Isabel Campoy and Alma Flor Ada have written more than a hundred books each and each has translated many books also. But they enjoy writing and translating books in collaboration. It's great fun!

Sobre las traductoras

F. Isabel Campoy y Alma Flor Ada han escrito más de cien libros cada una, y cada una también ha traducido muchos libros. Pero les encanta cuando pueden escribir o traducir libros entre las dos. ¡Es muy divertido!

For information about permission to reproduce selections from this book, please write to Permissions, Houghton Mifflin Harcourt Publishing Company
215 Park Avenue South NY NY 10003.

www.hmhbooks.com

First Green Light Readers edition 2000
Green Light Readers is a trademark of Houghton Mifflin Harcourt Publishing Company, registered in the United States of America and/or other jurisdictions.

SANDPIPER and the SANDPIPER logo are trademarks of Houghton Mifflin Harcourt Publishing Company.

The Library of Congress has cataloged an earlier edition as follows:
Crummel, Susan Stevens.
Tumbleweed stew/Susan Stevens Crummel; illustrated by Janet Stevens.
p. cm.
"Green Light Readers."
Summary: Jack Rabbit tricks the other animals into helping him make a pot of tumbleweed stew.
[1. Rabbits—Fiction. 2. Tricks—Fiction.]   I. Stevens, Janet, ill.   II. Title.
PZ7.C88845Tu 2000
[E]—dc21   99-50803

ISBN 0-547-25260-5
ISBN 0-547-25261-2 (pb)

Printed in China
SCP 10 9 8 7
4500463499

Ages 5–7
Grades: 1–2
Guided Reading Level: G–1
Reading Recovery Level: 17

Green Light Readers
For the reader who's ready to GO!

Five Tips to Help Your Child Become a Great Reader

1. Get involved. Reading aloud to and with your child is just as important as encouraging your child to read independently.

2. Be curious. Ask questions about what your child is reading.

3. Make reading fun. Allow your child to pick books on subjects that interest her or him.

4. Words are everywhere—not just in books. Practice reading signs, packages, and cereal boxes with your child.

5. Set a good example. Make sure your child sees YOU reading.

Why Green Light Readers Is the Best Series for Your New Reader

● Created exclusively for beginning readers by some of the biggest and brightest names in children's books

● Reinforces the reading skills your child is learning in school

● Encourages children to read—and finish—books by themselves

● Offers extra enrichment through fun, age-appropriate activities unique to each story

● Incorporates characteristics of the Reading Recovery® program used by educators

● Developed with Harcourt School Publishers and credentialed educational consultants

Colección Luz Verde

¡Para los lectores que están listos para AVANZAR!

Cinco sugerencias para ayudar a que su niño se vuelva un gran lector

1. Participe. Leerle en voz alta a su niño, o leer junto con él, es tan importante como animar al niño a leer por sí mismo.

2. Exprese interés. Hágale preguntas al niño sobre lo que está leyendo.

3. Haga que la lectura sea divertida. Permítale al niño elegir libros sobre temas que le interesen.

4. Hay palabras en todas partes, no sólo en los libros. Anime a su niño a practicar la lectura leyendo carteles, anuncios e información, como en las cajas de cereales.

5. Dé un buen ejemplo. Asegúrese de que su niño vea que USTED lee.

Por qué esta serie es la mejor para los lectores que comienzan

- Ha sido creada exclusivamente para los niños que empiezan a leer, por algunos de los más brillantes e importantes creadores de libros infantiles.

- Refuerza las habilidades de lectura que su niño está aprendiendo en la escuela.

- Anima a los niños a leer libros de principio a fin, por sí solos.

- Ofrece actividades de enriquecimiento, entretenidas y apropiadas para la edad del lector, creadas para cada cuento.

- Incorpora características del programa Reading Recovery usado por educadores.

- Ha sido desarrollada por la división escolar de Harcourt y por consultores educativos acreditados.

Look for more bilingual Green Light Readers!
Éstos son otros libros de la serie bilingüe Colección Luz Verde

LEVEL/NIVEL

1

Daniel's Pet/Daniel y su mascota
Alma Flor Ada/G. Brian Karas

Sometimes/Algunas veces
Keith Baker

The Big, Big Wall/ No puedo bajar
Reginald Howard/Ariane Dewey/ Jose Aruego

Big Brown Bear/El gran oso pardo
David McPhail

Big Pig and Little Pig/Cerdo y Cerdito
David McPhail

What Day Is It?/¿Qué día es hoy?
Alex Moran/Daniel Moreton

LEVEL/NIVEL

2

Daniel's Mystery Egg/El misterioso huevo de Daniel
Alma Flor Ada/G. Brian Karas

Digger Pig and the Turnip/Marranita Poco Rabo y el nabo
Caron Lee Cohen/Christopher Denise

Chick That Wouldn't Hatch/El pollito que no quería salir del huevo
Claire Daniel/Lisa Campbell Ernst

Get That Pest!/¡Agarren a ése!
Erin Douglas/Wong Herbert Yee

Catch Me If You Can!/¡A que no me alcanzas!
Bernard Most